BETWEEN TWO FIRES SERIES
Book 1 of 5

SHATTERED CROWNS

The Weight of Beautiful Ruins

Chelsey Morgan

The Amazon Endure typeface was designed by 2K/DENMARK in 2025.
Template id: ST-414D415A-25-A01
Printed in The United States.
ISBN: 979-8-90417-693-8

DEDICATION

I dedicate this book and all of my book series to my kids. They watched me go thru hell and back while still having a smile on face and making sure that they were safe, alive, fed, dressed and happy. These books are for you guys.
-Mommy loves you always.

TABLE OF CONTENTS

PROLOGUE

Now

There is a particular quality of silence in the hours just before dawn that I have come to know intimately. Not the peaceful kind — not the silence of rest or surrender or dreamless sleep. I mean the wide-awake, three-in-the-morning silence where the house breathes around you and your mind refuses the mercy of stillness. The kind where you lie there cataloguing everything you should have seen sooner.

I know this silence the way I know my own hands.

My name is Celeste Monroe. I am thirty years old. I am five feet two inches of Black woman forged in the particular fire of a Southern upbringing, two marriages that each ended in their own brand of wreckage, a mother who could burn a room down with nothing but a mood and a well-timed phone call, and one man — one specific, particular, Haitian man — who spent nearly three years teaching me, painstakingly and without apology, that a beautiful lie told consistently enough can feel exactly like the truth.

I have three daughters and two sons. Amara is eleven — eleven going on forty-five, with her father's pragmatism and my mother's terrifying perceptiveness. Imani is nine, obsessed with marine animals in the particular way of a child who has decided her purpose early. Zora is six, made entirely of spinning and song. Elijah is five, solemn and interior and watchful — the child who sees everything and says only what he means. And Henry — my youngest, my baby — is three, and has been the most effective antidepressant I have ever had access to, because that child performs for every single room he enters and has never once let a sad silence stand unchallenged.

Five children. My whole heart, distributed across five separate, breathing, chaos-generating people. They are the reason I get up every morning when every morning gives me new reasons to stay in bed.

I am writing this down because I need to understand it. Because the story I am about to tell you — the story of Édouard Pierre, and what he did to me, and what I did to myself, and what almost happened on a wet highway — is a story I have been too ashamed to say out loud until now. Shame, I have learned, is the primary mechanism by which the wrong people keep you silent.

So I am going to be loud. Even if it is only on paper. Even if only you

can hear it.
I want to start at the beginning. Not the accident — that comes later. Not the moment I found out about the women — that comes later too. I want to start on a hot August night when I was sitting in my mother's house with five children asleep in arrangements that defied the laws of physics, and my best friend Kezia downloaded an app onto my phone that changed the next nearly three years of my life in ways I am still accounting for.
I want you to know what brought me to that August night first, because context is everything.
On the day I turned thirty, my husband was arrested.
Not a warning, not a buildup I could point to and say I saw it coming from there. One moment I was standing in my kitchen in a dress I had bought for my own birthday dinner, and the next moment there were police lights outside my door. Marcus Sr. — father of my youngest son, a man I had loved with a ferocity I mistook for depth — was arrested for domestic violence. And our landlord, upon being informed by authorities of the situation, exercised the lease clause that allowed him to remove us from the property.
On my thirtieth birthday, I became a woman without a home.
I packed my children and what I could carry and moved into my mother's one-bedroom house in the middle of a Georgia summer. Five children. One bathroom. My mother's moods. The specific, relentless heat of a Georgia August compressed into a space that was never built for seven people.
That is the context. That is what I was carrying when Kezia sat down next to me three months later and told me I needed to remember I was still alive.
I swiped right on a man whose profile said: I love dogs. I love kids. I love being in the house. I play video games. I read. I love art and crafts. I am an introvert just looking for my match in COD.
Lord. I want to go back and hold that version of myself. I want to sit with her in the heat of that house and say: baby, you are not broken. You are tired, and you are hopeful, and those are not the same thing. And the person you are about to meet is going to use both against you.
But she wouldn't have listened. She needed to feel something. She needed to believe that this time, finally, the feeling was real.
This is the story of what it cost her to find out it wasn't.
And this is the story of how she survived it anyway.

PART ONE

THE BEAUTIFUL DECEPTION

"Wolves learn quickly which wounds are already open." —
Anonymous

CHAPTER ONE
August: The App, The Profile, The Swipe

The August that changed everything started the same way all my Augusts had started since my second marriage ended: loud, hot, crowded, and short on space.

I was thirty years old and living in my mother's house with five children. My second husband — Marcus Sr., father of my youngest, Henry — had been arrested on the night of my birthday, and our landlord had wasted no time exercising the clause that put us out. So there I was: Celeste Monroe, marketing professional, mother of five, packed into a one-bedroom house in the middle of a Georgia summer with my mother, Darlene, whose particular brand of love has always come attached to conditions I never fully agreed to.

The house was small in the specific way of places that were never meant to hold this many people for this long. One bedroom, a kitchen that fit one person standing straight, and a living room we had converted into sleeping quarters by necessity. Amara and Imani shared the pull-out couch. Zora and Elijah shared an air mattress. Henry slept in a Pack 'n Play in the corner. I slept in the bedroom with my mother, which is its own particular intimacy I would not recommend to anyone without an extremely resilient nervous system.

We had been there for three months when Kezia arrived on a Thursday evening with a bottle of Moscato and the energy of someone who has decided to fix something.

"Celeste Monroe," she said, settling onto the pull-out couch with the authority of a woman who has been my best friend since we were twelve years old, "you are thirty years old and you are in your mama's house eating cereal out of the box because you are too tired to cook."

"The cereal is organic," I said.

"You have not been on a date since before Marcus got locked up."

"I have been in litigation, relocation, and solo parenting five children."

"And you are still the most beautiful woman in any room you walk into, and you are sitting here in your mother's living room like you are done." She poured two glasses of Moscato. "You are not done. You are paused. There is a difference."

I took the glass. I was tired in the specific way of someone who has been managing emergencies for so long that emergency has become the baseline. Kezia knows this about me. She also knows, with the precision of twenty-two years of friendship, exactly when to push.

"I am not downloading a dating app," I said.

"I know," she said, and downloaded one onto my phone while I was drinking.

I gave her the look. The look that has never, in two decades of friendship, worked on her.

She handed my phone back and said, "One month. You don't have to marry anyone. You just have to remember that you're still alive."

The children were asleep. My mother was in the bedroom. The house was as quiet as a space containing five children ever gets. I sat in the heat with my Moscato and my phone and the specific loneliness of being surrounded by people who need you and still feeling, in the middle of all that need, entirely alone.

I opened the app.

I was not looking for anyone in particular. I was scrolling with the absent curiosity of someone killing time at the edge of a decision they have not fully made.

His profile was not the flashiest. Some of the men I passed had professional photographs with studio lighting and practiced smiles. His photo looked candid, slightly off-center — him laughing at something outside the frame, head turned to catch the light on the angle of his jaw. Deep brown skin, close-cropped hair. The laugh looked genuine. In a landscape of performed approachability, genuine was notable.

His bio: I love dogs. I love kids. I love being in the house. I play video games. I read. I love art and crafts. I am an introvert just looking for my match in COD.

I stared at that for a moment. No list of accomplishments. No curated catalog of attractive qualities. No pickup energy. Just: this is who I am, this is what I love, come find me in the game. I played Call of Duty. I had put it in my own profile as a joke, thinking no one would mention it. This man led with it.

I swiped right at 11:47 on a Thursday night in August.

By 11:49 we were a match.

He messaged first.

Hey. Wow you are stunning. I read your profile. So you play Call of Duty? What's your gamer tag? I would like to play with you.

I read that message three times. Looking for the script. Because I know how men talk when they want something. This was the first time on this app that a man was not asking for sex or trying to meet up so quickly. This man was genuinely interested in a hobby of mine and getting to know me.

Or so I thought.

Celeste, I typed back. And yours?

Édouard. But most people call me Ed.

Do you prefer Ed?

I prefer whatever you want to call me.

I smiled. Alone in my mother's hot living room at midnight, with five children asleep in artful arrangements around me, I smiled at a stranger's text and felt something loosen in my chest like a knot that had been pulled too tight for too long.

We talked until 2 a.m.

About Call of Duty first — he played seriously, had an actual clan, wanted to know my stats. I told him I was decent and he said prove it with the easy confidence of someone who expects to be surprised. We talked about food. He cooked Haitian food; I described my grandmother's recipes. We argued affectionately about rice versus cornbread. About music. About Atlanta versus Port-au-Prince. About the particular exhaustion of being fully alive in spaces that only want part of you.

He asked about my children. I mentioned them early, always, as a kind of sorting mechanism — five is a number that moves some men toward the door before they have even found their coat. He did not move toward the door. He asked their ages and their names and when I told him about Henry's three-year-old theatrical tendencies, he said, "That child is going to either change the world or exhaust it completely," and I laughed so hard I had to clap a hand over my mouth.

He made me laugh in my mother's living room at midnight. For the first time in a very long time, I felt like a whole person and not just a system of functions keeping five other people alive.

When we said goodnight, I set my phone down and sat very still.

I felt it. The particular, dangerous feeling of actual interest. The kind that moves through you like weather.

"Be careful," I told myself, in the voice I use when I am being truly sincere with myself.

He texted me good morning at 7:03 the next day.

He called the day after that during his lunch break, and the call lasted an hour and a half. He told me about his family in Haiti, his mother still in Port-au-Prince, his coming to the United States at twenty-two. He told me about his work in construction management, running his own crew, the specific pride of a man who has built something with his hands. He told me about his two dogs — both pit mixes he had raised from puppies, with names pulled from Haitian history. He talked about them the way people talk about the things they are genuinely responsible for and genuinely love.

He talked about them like family.

I should have paid closer attention to that.

CHAPTER TWO

August into September: Every Morning, Like Clockwork

He called every morning at eight o'clock.

I need you to understand what this means — not as a romantic gesture but as structural fact. Édouard Pierre called me every morning at eight o'clock on the dot when he was on a job site, from the dock, sometimes with machinery humming in the background, sometimes from his truck before the crew arrived. Every single morning, without exception, for the first months of our knowing each other. Before I had met him in person. Before anything had been named or made official. Eight a.m., my phone would ring, and his voice would be there.

This is what consistency looks like when it is weaponized. It builds something in your nervous system. It rewires your mornings around an expectation. It creates, over time, a feeling of being held by the simple fact of being reliably thought of. And when you are a woman who has spent years not being reliably thought of — who has been managing and surviving and holding everything together alone — that eight o'clock call becomes more than a call. It becomes evidence. It becomes proof of something you have been quietly, desperately hoping was still possible.

I know all of this now. I am telling it to you now so that when I describe what came later, you understand the weight of what was being dismantled.

We played games online together in the evenings — Call of Duty, word games, whatever kept us on the phone with a reason besides the talking, though the talking was always the real thing. He was competitive in a way that made me competitive. He would trash-talk with the ease of someone who had been doing it since childhood, and I would match him, and somewhere in the matching I stopped performing ease and started actually having it.

On weekends I drove to his place. This requires context: I was living at my mother's, and I was not bringing a man I had met on an app — a man still being figured out — into my mother's house with my five children. My children's security was not a variable I experimented

with. So I went to him.
He lived an hour from me, in his own house. Well — at least I thought it was his at first. More on that later.
The first time I drove there I sat in my car outside for five full minutes reminding myself I was a grown woman who had survived substantially harder things than a Saturday afternoon with a man she had been talking to for three weeks.
When I knocked on the door, his mother answered.
I was not expecting to meet her on our first visit. I was kind and respectful to her, and she was kind and respectful to me. It was awkward — undeniably awkward — but I brushed it off, thinking perhaps this was part of their culture, that it was normal for a Haitian mother to be so present in her adult son's space. Boy was I in for a surprise about their relationship.
When he came down to meet me, he looked like his photo, which sounds like a low bar but is not always cleared. He was tall — six-one, maybe six-two — with the particular physical ease of a man who works with his body and is comfortable in it. He was wearing a plain white t-shirt and sweatpants and he was barefoot.
His mother had made actual Haitian food. Griot, rice and peas, plantains. The house smelled extraordinary, and it was clean and well organized. He was polite and soft-spoken and smelled good too. Another thing I noticed was that he was completely unbothered about his mother meeting a woman he had met on an app three weeks ago — the relaxed quality of someone who is actually listening rather than waiting for their turn.
We ate at the kitchen table and talked for six hours. His two dogs circled us with the low-key surveillance of animals who are suspicious of new people and then, incrementally, decided I was acceptable. By the time I left that evening, both dogs were at my feet and Éd was walking me to my car with the unhurried quality of someone simply living an evening rather than performing the end of one.
"Same time next week?" he said.
"Same time next week," I said.
I drove home playing music louder than I usually do and feeling something I had almost forgotten — the particular lightness of anticipation. Of having something to look forward to.
Every Saturday for the rest of that month I drove to his house. We played Call of Duty for hours, trash-talking at each other across the screen the way people do when they are actually comfortable together. We cooked sometimes, or his mother had already cooked, and we ate

and talked past midnight. I drove home in the dark feeling full in a way that had nothing to do with food.

In between Saturdays: every day. He called at eight from the job site. Texted during his lunch. Called in the evenings, sometimes briefly, sometimes for hours. When my day was difficult — a hard morning with my mother, a challenge with one of the kids, the grinding anxiety of too many things and too little space — he was there. Not with solutions I hadn't asked for. Just present. Just listening in the particular way of someone who is actually processing rather than waiting for their turn.

Around week six, I remember thinking that I hadn't felt this seen in a relationship since — honestly, I couldn't remember since when. Which told me something. Which I should have paid more attention to.

Because the thing about feeling seen, after a long time of not being seen, is that it makes you want to protect the feeling. It makes you cautious about questioning it, about doing anything that might disrupt the particular warmth of finally, finally being looked at directly.

He hadn't called me his girlfriend. Nothing had been named. But we talked every day and saw each other every weekend and I had started, quietly and without announcement, to feel like his.

That was the first assumption I made.

It would not be the last.

CHAPTER THREE

October: The Friend From New York

The first sign that something was off came in October, in the form of a friend nobody told me was coming.

That is the part I want you to hold onto: I did not know the friend was arriving. There was no warning, no casual mention in the days prior, no "hey, my boy from New York is coming down this weekend." The friend's visit was revealed to me on the day he arrived — while Éd was on the phone with me from the job site, his tone slightly different than usual, I heard a commotion in the background and he said, "Hold on, my boy just landed."

Just landed. As in: the plane had just touched down. As in: this had been planned for some time and I had not been told.

I filed that away.

The night the friend arrived, Éd called me from the job site the way he always did. The friend had come along to the site — which explained the slightly different energy on the call, a little more distracted, a little split. We were in the middle of a conversation when I heard a voice in the background ask Éd who he was talking to.

And Éd said: "My homegirl."

Two words. My homegirl.

I want to be precise about what happened in my chest when I heard that. It wasn't a dramatic crash. It was more like something quiet and load-bearing gave way. A small structural failure. We had been talking every single day for two months. I drove to him every weekend. I had eaten food his mother cooked and let myself, carefully, begin to feel something. And to his friend — to the person he was putting on a face for — I was a homegirl.

I hung up the phone.

Not dramatically. Not with words. I just set it down. Sat with what I had heard and tried to decide what it meant. Maybe I had been building a story in my head that didn't match the one he was living.

The problem was that two months of eight a.m. calls and six-hour Saturdays and being listened to like I mattered did not feel like the curriculum of a friendship. It felt like something being built. Something that, I now realized, I had been building alone.

He didn't call back that night. Which had never happened before — even on busy days, even when he was tired, there had always been a check-in. That night: nothing.

The next morning: no eight o'clock call. I stared at my phone at eight-oh-five like it had done something personally offensive. I texted at eight-fifteen: good morning. Received a response forty-five minutes later: busy, talk later.

He did not call that day. Or the next morning. When I finally reached him on the second day, he was distracted in the way of someone whose attention is genuinely elsewhere — kept saying hold on, give me a second, I'll call you back — and then he wouldn't.

I kept my feelings internal and functioning. I told myself this was the friend's visit. Temporary disruption. He would return to normal when the friend left.

Then came the FaceTime.

A few evenings into the friend's visit, I was in a store — picking up something for the kids — when my phone rang with a FaceTime request from Éd. In the entire time we had been talking, he had never once FaceTimed me. Not once. We talked on the phone, we texted. FaceTime had never been part of the pattern.

I answered because I was surprised enough that caution didn't arrive in time.
He looked off. His eyes were slightly unfocused in the specific way of someone who has been drinking more than they usually do. There was noise behind him. He was louder than his usual register, with the particular loose-limbed energy of someone not entirely inside their own body at the moment.
"Hey," he said, like it was nothing. Like we hadn't spoken properly in days.
"We're about to go out. Strip club, then a comedy show. You know how it is."
I did not know how it was. In two months of daily conversation and weekly visits, Éd had presented himself as profoundly unbothered by nightlife — a house person, a stay-in person, an introvert who had said so in his very first message to me. He had never once mentioned clubs or bars. He had presented himself as the exact opposite of a man who went to strip clubs on weeknights.
And here he was, slightly drunk, headed to a strip club, like that version of himself had simply never existed.
"I thought you were coming to the hotel this weekend," I said. I had already booked it — our usual arrangement, since I wasn't bringing him to my mother's house.
He blinked. He had completely forgotten.
"Oh yeah. I'll come through."
He came through very late. Late enough that "coming through" was barely the right description. He smelled like a strip club — cigarette smoke and perfume and the specific close-quarters smell of a room full of women and alcohol — and had clearly attempted a shower that had done incomplete work on any of it.
I said nothing about where he had been or what he smelled like. I was performing composure with every resource I had, because I had decided, in the hours between his FaceTime and his arrival, that I was not going to be the woman who made scenes.
What he said, at some point before morning, was that I smelled bad. That my body smelled bad. He said it casually, almost offhandedly, in the tone of someone who believes they are being honest rather than cruel.
He had arrived smelling like a strip club and a shower that hadn't worked, and he had the audacity — the specific, breathtaking audacity — to tell me that I smelled. Whatever he had carried in on his body, he redirected onto mine.

I went very still in the way that is not calm but is the space before calm.
In the morning he left to go back to his friend, and for the remainder of that visit I heard from Éd in fragments. Half-conversations. Texts that said hold on and calls that said I'll call you back and did not.
The moment — the exact moment — his friend's plane left Atlanta, Éd called me at eight a.m. On the dot. Like a switch had been flipped. Like the previous two weeks had been a weather event that had passed, and we were back to normal, and I was supposed to simply step back into our rhythm as though I hadn't spent two weeks pressing bruises.
He even talked about the visit fondly. Told stories from it. Laughed about things his friend had said. I listened and I responded and I kept the thing that was eating at me pressed below the surface where it couldn't reach his good mood.
But it was eating at me. Something about the way he had become a different person during that visit — the strip clubs, the drinking, the FaceTime out of nowhere, the forgetting about the hotel — and then snapping back to himself the moment his friend left, as though I was only accessible when no one else was watching.
I did not say any of this. I kept moving.
I have regretted that more than I can accurately quantify.

CHAPTER FOUR

October into November: The Children Conversation, The Ghost, and Jimmy

The children conversation happened about a week after his friend flew back to New York.
We were on the phone in the evening, one of those long calls that meanders the way good conversations do, when the subject of children came up. He said it just like that, in the middle of a sentence: "I think I only want one kid. I'm not built for a lot."
I held the phone and said, carefully: "I have five. So where does that put us?"
The pause before he answered was longer than it should have been for a man who had been calling me every morning for two months.
"I'm talking to you, aren't I?"
That was the whole answer. As though the fact of ongoing contact

was sufficient response to the question of whether five children were a dealbreaker for a man who had just declared himself a one-child man. As though I should be satisfied with the fact of his continued presence rather than the substance of what that presence meant.

After his response we sat on the phone in silence for what seemed like forever. Then I asked him if he was uncomfortable and he replied, "Yes." I then told him that I was going to bed and would talk to him tomorrow. He didn't even respond. As I laid there, I kept repeating his answer in my head. After some time I sent him a text: "I have five kids. You only want one. And you don't want a lot of kids? Maybe we are not meant for each other." I know sending this was kind of harsh, but I expected him to at least respond.

He didn't respond.

Not that day. Not the next morning — no eight o'clock call. Not a text, not anything.

I had never in my life been with someone who simply went silent in conflict. Both of my ex-husbands, whatever else they were, were present in disagreement. They argued, they defended, they over-explained. They did not disappear. This disappearance was new to me, and it was disorienting in the specific way of something that gives you no surface to push against.

After two days I said to Kezia: I think we're done.

"He didn't say that," Kezia said.

"He didn't say anything. That's worse."

On the third day he texted: We're not done. I've just been busy.

Busy. Two days of silence after a direct question about the viability of our situation, and the answer was busy. I absorbed it and moved on, the way I had been doing my whole life, because some habits are grooved too deep to interrupt without a reason more compelling than a single word text.

What he offered instead of a real answer was a new story: he had an annual tradition of visiting his old college campus — something he did every year around this time. He mentioned this as explanation for the recent unavailability, which raised the immediate question of why he hadn't mentioned it in advance since it was apparently a yearly tradition. I did not ask that question.

Here was this Jimmy being mentioned again. This time for a road trip to their college. I found out that they met in college and had been friends since. He was the one who occupied a steady, load-bearing space in Éd's life that I was only now beginning to map.

"You and Jimmy are close," I said.

"He's my boy," Éd said, in a tone that closed the subject.

I filed Jimmy away and kept moving.

The incident that led to us becoming official happened in a way I am not proud of, and I am going to tell it plainly because the whole point of this accounting is honesty.

He had told me one evening he was going to Jimmy's to play video games — they did this regularly. He texted when he got there, then went quiet. An hour passed. Then two. I texted and got nothing back. Called and it rang to voicemail. Twice.

I want to be honest about what happened in me during those hours. It wasn't rational. It was the residue of the New York friend visit, the homegirl comment, the children conversation, and two days of silence — the specific accumulation of small unaddressed things that had settled into a low-grade anxiety about where I actually stood.

I called a man I had met briefly at a Walmart some weeks prior — someone who had given me his number in the way men do, and I had kept it in the way women do when they are not entirely sure of the situation they are in and want to keep their options open. I called him. I went to see him. And yes — I will say it plainly — I slept with him.

When Éd finally called back, I was home. He asked what I had been doing. I told him I had been hanging out with a friend. I did not specify which friend or what the hanging out involved.

He found out, or got close enough to finding out, the following day. I still do not know exactly how. But his energy shifted — became taut and territorial in a way it hadn't been before — and he asked me directly whether anything had happened with the guy from Walmart.

I said no.

This was a lie. I am not proud of it. But the context was: a man who had not confirmed what we were, who had called me a homegirl to his friend, who had disappeared for two days, who had treated the previous two weeks as though I was only accessible when no one more interesting was present. I was not his girlfriend. I had not been told I was. And yet I was expected to behave as though I was.

That contradiction is its own commentary.

The result of his jealousy — and he was jealous, visibly, in a way he had not been before — was that he asked me to be exclusive. Formally, directly, during sex — yeah, I know, don't judge me. He wanted to make it official. He wanted to know I was his.

I said yes. Because I had wanted to say yes for months and the only thing standing between me and yes was the fact that he hadn't asked. He was now asking.

But I kept my options quietly. Not as a statement — just as a fact. Because I didn't fully trust him yet, and the keeping was the part of me that still remembered how to protect herself. I told myself I would let the options go when he gave me genuine reason to.

When he became consistent — truly, demonstrably consistent — I let them go.

And then I stopped trusting my instincts. Because the consistency felt like proof, and proof, I had decided, was the thing I had been waiting for.

I was wrong about that too.

CHAPTER FIVE

November: My Own House, and the Beginning of Something Real

Three months after meeting Éd, I got my own place.

I cannot fully describe what it meant to have my own space again. A door that was mine. A kitchen where I could spread out. A living room where my children could leave their things without apologizing for taking up space. Bedrooms — actual bedrooms — where each of my kids could sleep in a real bed and not an arrangement born of necessity.

My mother came with us. This was not romantic but practical: she helped with the children when my work required it, and she needed stability that her own place was not reliably providing, and despite the complexity of our relationship, she is my mother and we make it work.

The house was a four-bedroom, two-and-a-half bath, which felt like luxury compared to what we had left.

Éd helped us move in. When he walked through it, it was with the quiet appreciation of someone who understood what having your own space meant. My kids got to meet him for the first time. They loved him right away. My mother, on the other hand, was quiet and distant and ran upstairs. That would be the beginning of their hatred for each other.

With that first visit, it became the beginning of the weekend visits that would define the next two years. He would come on Saturdays, sometimes staying into Sunday, and we would exist in the ordinary domesticity of a couple — the children loud and alive around us, my home finally feeling like a home. The children grew accustomed to him. Amara continued her detective assessment. Imani told him increasingly elaborate facts about marine animals. Zora performed for him regularly. Elijah sat near him in wordless endorsement. Henry commandeered his lap and called him "Ed-man," which was the highest honor a three-year-old could bestow.

We were, by any visible measurement, a couple building something.

What I did not yet see was that the building was uneven. That I was providing the foundation while he was providing the architecture, and that what looked like a shared project was, from his side of the table, something considerably more provisional.

But in November, in my own house with my children in real beds, I allowed myself to not see that yet.

I was happy. Genuinely, simply, straightforwardly happy.

I should have written it down. Happiness that specific is worth documenting when you have it.

CHAPTER SIX

Year One: The Pattern Beneath the Pattern

The first year of being official was the best year. I am saying this without sarcasm and without revisionism. It was consistent, and consistency, when you have been through what I had been through, is not a small thing. It is the thing.

He called every morning. He came every weekend. He knew my children. He made me laugh. He listened in the way of someone who was genuinely present, who catalogued what I told him and brought it back at unexpected moments in ways that made me feel, continuously, like I was being held in someone's careful attention.

But the pattern beneath the pattern was always there. I simply did not have the language for it yet.

Jimmy.

Jimmy was a consistent background presence in our relationship that I kept trying to fit into the box marked "close male friendship" because that was the box that made the most sense and required the least examination. He called during our dinners — not always, but often enough that I began to register the consistency of it. He texted during our Saturday afternoons, and Éd would step away to respond, phone angled slightly away from me in a way that was subtle enough to be deniable.

Once, I was in the kitchen getting water when I heard Éd in the living room on the phone, and the register of his voice was different. Lower. More intimate. The specific quietness of someone speaking in a private frequency. When I came back in, the call ended fairly quickly and he said, "That was Jimmy," in the preemptive way of someone who knows they are about to be asked.

I noted it. I did not ask about it.

The other pattern I began to notice was the long phone calls with his male friends — rambling conversations that could go on for an hour or more, during which he would put me on hold and come back and put me on hold again. Once, I was on hold for twenty-two minutes. I know the exact number because I was watching the clock. When he came back he acted as though the pause had been minor, the way you act when you don't think the other person is keeping track.

I was keeping track. I had been keeping track my whole life. Women who grow up in unstable environments count minutes. We track the weather because we learned early that the weather matters.

The marijuana was not something I knew about in year one. He was careful, at least initially. The first time I smelled it on him, I mentioned it and he shrugged it off: "I was around somebody who was smoking. Nothing."

"I didn't know you smoked," I said.

"I don't, really," he said.

This was the first explicit lie I can identify in retrospect. Not dramatic. Not about anything that should matter enormously. But the first time I watched him say something factually untrue, smoothly, without hesitation, with the ease of someone who had long since made peace with casual dishonesty.

I accepted the explanation and moved on.

Something else began in year one, quietly and almost imperceptibly: the expansion of his expectations of me. He had always appreciated that I cooked — I enjoyed it, it was never a chore — but somewhere in year one it shifted from appreciation to expectation. Meals were assumed rather than received. If I hadn't cooked when he arrived, there was a quality to his manner that was not quite displeasure but adjacent to it. He began to bring more of his things to my house. Not as a discussed decision — nothing was ever decided. But his presence in my space became more material over time. A jacket. A phone charger that became permanent. His dogs staying over on weekends. His gaming setup installed in my living room without asking, as though the house were already his.

I noticed all of it. I absorbed it.

The year, on the whole, was good. I insist on this not as delusion but as accuracy. The calls were real. The laughter was real. The way he looked at me across my kitchen table like I was the most interesting thing in whatever room he happened to be in — that was real, or felt real, which in terms of its effect on my nervous system is the same thing.

I needed to stay in the real and stop looking at what was underneath it. I was very good at that.

PART TWO

THE SLOW UNRAVELING

"The truth does not require your belief to exist. It simply waits." – Unknown

CHAPTER SEVEN
Year Two: Hairline Cracks

The second year was the year the cracks appeared.

Not catastrophically. Not in a way that demanded immediate accounting. Just hairline fractures — the kind you notice in a wall and tell yourself are cosmetic, are structural settling, are nothing. The kind you learn to see around rather than address, because addressing them would require you to consider what they mean about the foundation.

His cancelations increased. Where in year one he had arrived on Saturdays with the reliability that had rewired my mornings, in year two the arrivals became conditional. Work ran over. He was tired. He needed "peace" — this word he began to use with increasing frequency, as though my house and my children and my presence were things that disrupted rather than provided it. He'd text on a Friday: I just need to decompress this weekend. And I would rearrange my Saturday around his absence and say okay, rest up.

I said okay more times than I should have.

The Jimmy situation also escalated in year two. There was an evening I will not forget. I was on the phone with Éd — we were mid-conversation, something substantive — when his phone beeped with another call.

"Hold on. It's Jimmy."

He clicked over. I held. Eleven minutes.

When he came back, his energy was different — quieter, more contained, with the quality of someone who has just put down something heavier than what they're now holding. He did not explain what Jimmy had needed. He picked up our conversation as though the pause had been seconds.

"That was a long call," I said.

"He needed to talk," Éd said. "You know how Jimmy is."

I did not know how Jimmy was. I had met Jimmy exactly once. Every time I tried to ask a direct question about him, the answer was general. Every time Jimmy called, the response was immediate in a way that my calls were not always met with.

"You drop everything for him," I said, carefully, as an observation rather than an accusation.

"He's been through a lot," Éd said.

"You've never really told me about him."

"There's not much to tell. He's my boy. That's it."

That's it — with a door-closing finality I had learned not to push against. Because pushing produced nothing except a quality of irritation in Éd that he managed to make feel like my fault.

The calls with his other male friends followed the same pattern. Long, meandering conversations during which I would be put on hold and left there. Once I was on hold for twenty-two minutes. When he came back he acted as though the pause had been minor.

The marijuana became more visible in year two. He stopped being careful about it in my space. It went from something I smelled on him occasionally to something simply present — the smell of it on his clothes when he arrived, sometimes on his breath. He was matter-of-fact about it in a way that preempted objection: this was who he was. The introvert-stay-at-home version of himself that he had presented in year one had either been performed or aspirational, and it had not held.

The drinking followed the same arc. Not dramatic. Not falling-down impaired. Just the steady, consistent presence of alcohol in quantities he had not disclosed at the beginning. Beer in the evenings that became beer in the afternoons on weekends. The particular looseness that came with it.

He began to treat my house like a service. I want to be precise here. He didn't ask me to cook — he simply arrived and expected it, and if it wasn't there, the temperature in the room dropped two degrees. He would sit in my living room while my children were present and contribute to the atmosphere without contributing to the management of it. He occasionally criticized things — how I handled a situation with one of the kids, the temperature of food, something I had or hadn't done — in the light, almost-playful tone of someone who knows they are being critical but wants deniability. "I'm just saying." "Just an observation." "Don't get sensitive."

Don't get sensitive. I had heard this phrase in my mother's voice for thirty years. Hearing it in his voice should have told me something. It did tell me something. I put it away.

But the calls were still there. The good evenings still arrived. And every time I got close to a conclusion, a good evening would arrive and scramble the math.

This is how it works. You don't keep someone with consistent cruelty. You keep them with inconsistent kindness. The ratio matters. Too much cruelty and they leave. Too much kindness and there is nothing to escape. It is the alternation — the good enough, often enough — that keeps the door from closing.

He was very good at the ratio.

CHAPTER EIGHT
The Dog, Jimmy, and the Night My Brother Died

I need to tell you about the dog before I tell you about my brother, because the two events are braided together in my memory in a way I have never been able to separate.

Éd had two dogs — one a Jack Terrier and the other a Yorkie, both named after figures from Haitian history, both beloved in the way that dogs are beloved when someone has raised them from puppies and organized a portion of their identity around the responsibility. He talked about his dogs the way he talked about few other things: with uncomplicated, genuine pride.

The female — a Jack Russell terrier he had gotten separately, a small and extremely opinionated dog named for a Haitian poet — died on a Tuesday.

He called me that afternoon and I could hear it in his voice before he said a word — the specific hollowness of fresh grief, the quality of a person whose nervous system is trying to process a loss it didn't see coming. He told me she had been sick for a few years and he hadn't realized how sick she recently became when he he went to Canada. It was an experience he had not been prepared for.

I listened. I said the things you say. I offered to come over and he said not tonight — tonight he wanted Jimmy.

Jimmy came over that same evening. They did a small funeral service for the dog in the backyard, and then what Éd described to me later as a celebration of her life — the specific kind of grief ritual that is more about honoring what existed than mourning what is gone. He told me about it the next day with a warmth that was genuine, and I was glad he had had someone with him, and I noted, without pressing on it, that the someone had been Jimmy and not me.

He invited me over the following day. I went, and the house was quieter than usual, and he was subdued in the way of someone still moving through fresh grief. I stayed for the afternoon. We sat together in the particular comfortable silence of people who have learned to occupy the same space without filling it.

Two days after the dog died, my brother took his own life.

I am going to let that sentence stand alone for a moment, because it

deserves the space.
My brother — my younger brother, whom I had been worrying about for months in the specific, helpless way of someone who can see a person drowning from shore and cannot reach them — died by suicide on a Monday evening. I found out from his wife, who had been in contact with me for months leading up to this, and the sound she made when I answered the phone is a sound I carry in my body and will carry there until I don't carry anything anymore.
Éd was there with me at my house already.
I want to tell you what I needed in those hours. I needed someone to stay. I needed a body in the room, a presence that did not require me to perform okay, someone who would simply be there in the specific, unglamorous way of sitting next to a person who is in the middle of the worst thing.
He stayed for a few more hours. And then he left.
He said he would be back. He said he needed to handle something. He said he would check on me later.
He said he would return.
He did not come back that night.
He did not come back the next day.
He did not return to my house until a week later.
A week. My brother had just died by suicide, and the man I had been with for almost two years — who had been at my house nearly every weekend, who knew my children, who had eaten meals I cooked and slept in my bed — was absent for a week. Not completely silent: there were texts, brief ones, checking in, asking if I was okay. But he was not there. And I needed him to be there, and he was not, and I did not have the language yet to tell him what his absence cost me because I was in the middle of surviving something and language was not my primary resource.
When he came back a week later, he was warm. Attentive in the way he had been attentive in year one, as though the week had been a weather event that had passed and we were back to where we were before. He asked about my mother. He asked about the arrangements. He held me.
And I let him, because I needed to be held and he was there and the alternative was holding myself in the silence of a house that had just gotten significantly quieter.
I want to be precise about what I am not saying. I am not saying that grief has a correct timeline or that there is a prescribed way to show up for someone who is suffering. I know that. I have enough self-

awareness to understand that my need for presence in those days was specific and intense and not every person is equipped to meet that need.

What I am saying is: he was not equipped, and he did not tell me he was not equipped, and instead of saying I don't know how to be with this, he simply disappeared. And the disappearing told me something that I filed away and did not address because the filing and the not-addressing had become my primary mode of operation in this relationship.

The dog died on Tuesday. My brother died on Thursday. Jimmy came for the dog. No one came for me.

I have thought about that more than I would like to admit.

CHAPTER NINE
The Money App and the Birthday That Almost Wasn't

I found out about the first woman because of a money app.

He had wanted to send me some money — this was not unusual, he did this occasionally, nothing large but a gesture — and he used an app I didn't have on my phone. He mentioned the name of it. I downloaded it.

After I set up my account. I added him and that's when the transaction history populated.

His transaction history.

I want to be clear: this was not deliberate snooping. I was setting up an app at his suggestion, using my own phone number, and his financial history appeared because he had previously used this app from my phone or linked my number to his account in some logistical way he had not disclosed. The discovery was accidental. The information was not.

There was a name. A woman's name, appearing multiple times in his transaction history. Not once or twice — multiple payments over multiple months. The pattern was consistent enough to constitute a financial relationship. And one of the transactions carried a note that contained the word birthday. A birthday that was not mine. A birthday that landed on a date I recognized for a different reason.

My birthday. He had been late to my birthday dinner. He had texted an hour before — something about a job running over — and I had sat at the restaurant with Kezia and my children and reconfigured the table for his absence and told myself it was fine. He had arrived eventually, slightly distracted, and I had been glad he came and had not interrogated the lateness.

And on that same day — while I was at that restaurant with my children — he had sent another woman money. On my birthday.

I closed the app. I sat with what I knew.

I found her social media pages — turns out she was a massage therapist, and had an only fans.

So I asked him about her, presenting what I had found without accusation. Just: who is this person, and why are you sending her money?

He didn't miss a beat.

"That's my homegirl. I owe her money. I borrowed some cash a while back, I'm paying her back."

Homegirl. The word again. The same word he had used for me, to his friend from New York, in our early days. The word designed to be technically true and emotionally false simultaneously, to sit in the space between friendship and something more and mean whatever is most convenient.

"You sent her money on my birthday," I said.

"I didn't even know what day it was. I was paying her back. It was a coincidence."

He said it with complete steadiness. No hesitation, no over-explanation. The fluency of someone who has prepared for the question or told the story enough times to have made it smooth.

I did not believe him. I also could not prove otherwise. So I absorbed it and moved on.

But I started paying attention differently after that. Quietly, without announcement, without confrontation. I started noting things I had previously noted and then put away. I started building the file.

Later — through other means, over more time — the truth about this woman was confirmed. She was not a homegirl he owed money to. She was someone he was seeing. The "owed money" explanation was a performance for me. And the confirmation of this came only after more time had passed, more evidence had accumulated, and I had become someone who could no longer look away from what the evidence was saying.

I will get there.

CHAPTER TEN
The Night Everything Came to the Surface

The night I found out — really found out, confirmation rather than suspicion — I can reconstruct in precise detail because I have revisited it enough times that it is more documentation than memory.

He had been at my house for the weekend. Over the course of several months, a substantial number of his possessions had drifted gradually from his place to mine — until his clothes were in a portion of my closet, his speakers were against my living room wall, his gaming setup had been installed without asking, and his dogs had spent enough weekends at my house that they knew where their water bowl was. His dogs were there that night. His systems were there. His jacket, his shoes in the entryway.

He had told me earlier that day that he had a job — outdoor work, a renovation, and it had rained, and the job had run late, and he had pulled over at a gas station and fallen asleep in his truck rather than drive tired in the rain.

A reasonable story. Internally coherent. The kind designed to be reasonable, that accounts for the timeline in a way that doesn't leave obvious gaps.

I found out it was a lie through a source I am not going to name, because the source's identity is not the point. The point is that the timeline he gave me did not match where he had actually been.

He never came back to my house. So I drove to his house and moved all of his things out. Methodically, and with anger, I had gathered every item that was his in my house — the clothing, the speakers, the gaming setup, the jacket, the shoes, the personal things — and I had transported them to his house.

All of it. I took all of it.

Including his dogs. I took them with me and tied them up to his back door. I continued to call him and text him, and he wouldn't answer. That was it. I was done. — At least I thought I was.

The next morning I awoke to him knocking on my door. — There he was eyes bloodshot red, his stature unbalanced, he reeked of liquor and smoke. He asked where his things were and where were his dogs.

I told him his house. He left.

Soon after he arrived home he called me to tell me his dogs were gone. — with a fury that was so completely disproportionate to the circumstances of being caught in a lie that I still think about the architecture of his anger when I need to remember what kind of person he was.

I ignored his anger and I asked where he was — he said he fell asleep at a gas station and that his phone had died.

He called me a crazy bitch. — In heat-of-the-moment way. Deliberately. Repeatedly. With the specificity of someone who had decided this was the accurate description and was deploying it as fact. He said it about the situation with his belongings — which was his own fault, the consequence of him lying — and in the course of saying it he said nothing about the lie. The lie was not mentioned. The lie was not the event. I was the event. My response to his lie was the event.

He stopped talking to me after that call.

I found out he found his dogs not because he told me, but because I went to his house some days later with my dog to search for his dogs and heard them barking in the house.

They were fine. He had found them and said nothing to me, because telling me would have required acknowledging that I existed and had been waiting, and acknowledging my waiting would have meant acknowledging my right to be upset.

He started talking to me again approximately a week later. As though the week had been a weather event. As though I was supposed to simply resume because he had decided to.

I did not resume immediately. But I did resume. Because I had been trained, from my earliest consciousness, to believe that love is intermittent and conditional and that the withdrawal of warmth is a weather event rather than a choice, and that the right response to someone going cold is to wait for them to come back and be grateful when they do.

I resumed. We talked. He was warm again, briefly, in the way that followed every rupture — a return to form, a reminder of why I had stayed, a temperature that felt like confirmation that the good version was the real version.

I brought up the girl with the receipts I had quietly accumulated. He explained. The explanation was insufficient. I let it stand, not because I believed it but because I had run out of energy to disbelieve things that evening and I needed the conversation to be over.

He left my house and I sat in my living room and thought: I am still in this. I am sitting here, knowing what I know, and I am still in this.

I decided to understand that rather than be ashamed of it. Understanding it was the first step.

CHAPTER ELEVEN
Year Three: The Long, Slow Closing

Year three was the year I began to grieve the relationship while I was still inside it.

Grief is not always retrospective — sometimes it is present-tense, the feeling of losing something that is still technically there. Year three was that. A slow, conscious, ongoing loss accumulating even as I showed up to the relationship, continued the calls, remained.

He came to my house less. The excuses became the permanent backdrop: he was busy, tired, needed peace. Jimmy was a recurring explanation — they were hanging out, or Jimmy needed something, or he had plans with Jimmy made before he had made plans with me. The scheduling made clear, without his ever saying so explicitly, that Jimmy's claim on his time was unconditional in a way that mine was not.

There was a night I called him at ten p.m. and he didn't answer. Called again at ten-fifteen. Nothing. Texted. Nothing. At ten forty-five he texted back: with Jimmy, call you later. He did not call later. The next morning he called at eight as though nothing had happened.

"You texted me at ten forty-five," I said. "From your phone."

A pause. "I mean I was with Jimmy. I didn't want to be on the phone."

"You could have said that."

"I'm saying it now."

This was the grammar of year three. Every inconsistency had an explanation that was technically not a lie and was also not the truth. Every gap had a backstory just coherent enough to preclude confrontation. He had developed — or perhaps had always possessed and was simply using more freely — a way of rewriting events in real time, casually, without visible effort, that made my memory of them seem provisional.

My therapist calls this narrative control — the systematic replacement of your account of events with his, conducted with enough confidence and regularity that you eventually doubt your own record.

I am a precise woman. I remember things accurately. I have a detailed memory developed by a childhood that required it. And even I found myself, in year three, second-guessing things I had heard and seen and lived.

He disappeared for four days once — no calls, minimal texts, single-word responses. When he surfaced he said he had been dealing with a family situation he didn't want to talk about. I expressed concern and asked if there was anything I could do. He said no and changed the subject. The family situation was never mentioned again.

There were phone calls that ended abruptly — mid-conversation, he would say let me call you back and hang up, and the callback would arrive hours later or not until the following morning. Sometimes not at all.

The marijuana evenings became more frequent. He would arrive having already smoked, and the quality of his presence was slower, less available. He would be impatient with the children in a way that made my back go up. He never crossed a line with my children — I want to be precise about this — but there was a quality of tolerance that was not the same as welcome, and my children, who are perceptive in the ways that children with complicated histories are perceptive, felt it.

Amara told me once, without preamble, while we were washing dishes: "He's not as nice as he pretends to be."

"What do you mean?" I said, keeping my voice even.

"He's nice to your face but his face is doing something different," she said. "Like he's bored. Or like he thinks he's somewhere better than here."

My eleven-year-old. Reading a room I had been trying not to see.

"I hear you," I said.

"You should believe me," she said.

"I know," I said.

I did believe her. I just wasn't ready yet.

CHAPTER TWELVE
The Unlocked Phone

He left his phone on my kitchen counter one evening while he was in the shower.

I had not been looking for an opportunity. I had been standing at the counter and his phone, unlocked, lit up with a notification, and I looked at it the way you look at anything that illuminates in your peripheral vision.

What I saw on that screen made me pick up the phone.

What I found was not one woman.
It was not even just the woman from the money app, though she was there too, her thread active and recent and carrying in his messages to her a warmth I had not received in months.
It was multiple. Conversations that were not platonic, not ambiguous, not open to creative interpretation. Conversations with multiple women, each of which had the texture — the daily checking in, the specific attentiveness, the warmth deployed like a tool — of someone being deliberately maintained. What made it worse was he was chasing these women. He was dm'ing them being thirsty and acting like no one loved him. — Like he wasn't getting sex, food, love, and more from me and my children. The last message to a woman literally the night he arrived asking a woman if she liked his picture sent me down an emotional tunnel.
I read what I needed to read to confirm what I knew. I recorded it with my phone for proof later.
Then I put the phone down exactly where it had been.
The shower turned off.
I stood at the counter with my hands steady and my chest doing something I was not going to let become visible.
The thread that stayed with me — the one I have thought about most in the months since — was a woman with a child. A young child, she had written. And in the context of the thread she had, at one point, called Éd the father.
I am going to let that sentence stand alone because it deserves the space.
A woman had, in their conversation, referred to him as the father of her child. He had not corrected this. He had responded with the ease and familiarity of someone who accepted that designation.
I said nothing that evening. I waited — not because I was planning to, but because the scale of what I had found was so large that it required time to become real. Something too significant to absorb at full size has to arrive in stages.
I needed a week. A full week, alone with what I knew, before I said anything to anyone.
And then I confronted him.
Not with volume. Not with tears. With everything I had found, laid out clearly and sequentially, named and dated and specific. I presented it the way I would present a marketing analysis — here is the data, here is what the data indicates, here is the conclusion.
He started with denial. Then pivoted to my invasion of his phone. Then

came the reframe where my discovery was the event rather than the content of what I had discovered. Then a cold, flat quality that meant the performance was over.

I asked about the child.

He said he did not have a child.

“She is acting like he is your son.” I said.

"It's just complicated, Celeste. You don't need all of that right now."

As though information about whether the man I had spent nearly three years with might have fathered a child he had never mentioned was a matter of timing. As though there was a better moment for this.

I ended the conversation. Not the relationship — not yet, not with finality — but that specific evening. I had run out of language for what I was experiencing and I needed to be alone in it.

He left.

I sat in my living room for a long time and thought about three years. About the specific craftsmanship of a man who could maintain multiple versions of himself, each one sustained with daily contact and remembered details and deployed warmth, each one real enough to the person experiencing it to constitute something worth staying for.

I thought about all the mornings. Eight o'clock. Every morning, or close enough. The call from the job site, his voice arriving in my day before almost anything else.

All of it happening simultaneously on someone else's morning too.

PART THREE

THE ACCIDENT AND THE AFTERMATH

"Some people show you who they are not in how they love you, but in how they respond when you survive them." — Unknown

CHAPTER THIRTEEN
One Week Later: The Car, The Rain, The Impact

I need to preface this chapter by telling you that I have written it several times. Each time I stopped because I found myself dissociating in the middle of the writing — hands going cold, the words on the screen going distant, a cotton-wool quality descending over everything. This is that version. The one I made it through.

The accident happened one week after the confrontation.

In the days between the confrontation and the accident, we had moved through a strange, tentative space — the aftermath of revelation not yet fully processed. He had not apologized. I had not delivered an ultimatum. We were in the uneasy middle ground of two people who have seen each other clearly, perhaps for the first time, and are not yet sure what to do with the sight.

He called me on a morning and said he had a job interview. Something he was pursuing in a different field, and he was nervous about it in a way that was genuine enough that I felt, briefly, the old warmth. The person underneath the performance, reaching through.

He asked if I wanted to ride along. Like we used to do — in the early days, sometimes on his field jobs, I would ride with him, and we would talk the whole way there and back and the road itself felt like something.

I said yes. Because I thought we were possibly making up. Because hope, even severely damaged hope, continues operating on its own logic. Because I had said yes to this man so many times that yes had become my default setting in his presence.

The drive out was fine — he was focused, slightly nervous, and I talked at him the way I do when someone needs distraction from anxiety. We were okay in the car. It felt, briefly, like something it used to be.

The interview went well, he said, coming back to the car. He seemed lighter. We started the drive home.

It had begun to rain while he was inside. Not heavily — a steady, patient rain that made the roads reflective, the kind that looks manageable until you're moving through it.

His phone was in his hand.

I noticed it the way you notice things you have trained yourself to notice after years of watching someone's attention distribute itself to places that aren't you. His eyes were moving between the road and the screen, and this was a wet night and an active highway and I said his

name.
"Édouard. Put the phone down."
He made a sound — dismissive, the sound of someone who has found your concern tedious — and kept the phone in his hand.
"Édouard." Louder. "The road is wet. Put the phone down."
He glanced up. He glanced back down.
The other car came through the intersection.
What I remember: the sound of it. The way enormous sound is also very brief. The world going sideways. The airbag — the smell of it, chemical and burnt, a smell I will carry in my body for the rest of my life. Glass. Rain coming through where the window had been.
And then: stillness. The specific stillness of the moment after violence, when the world recalibrates around a new configuration of itself.
I was alive. I established this tentatively, with the specific astonishment of someone who was not certain until just now. My face was on the deflated airbag. My left arm was wet and warm in a way that meant bleeding. My ribs were a concentrated point of pain that I would later learn were bruised — three of them, on the right side.
I was alive.
He was already out of the car.
I could see him through what remained of the window. Standing in the rain, on his phone. I watched him for long enough to know with certainty that the first call he made after that car came through the intersection was not to emergency services.
He called someone else first. He stood in the rain, twenty feet from the car where I was sitting in glass and chemical smell and shock, and he called someone else.
I believe it was Jimmy. I cannot prove this. I am presenting it as what I believe, because it is consistent with everything I had observed and everything I would observe in the days that followed.
Emergency services were eventually called. An ambulance came. He came to the hospital, briefly, with the quality of someone fulfilling an obligation rather than responding to a crisis. He asked if I was okay in the way you ask someone when the answer is a formality. I told him I was okay. Concussion. Three bruised ribs. Laceration on my left forearm.
He left before they released me.
I called Kezia. She came immediately, in the way that Kezia comes when something is wrong — without questions, without delay, with the specific reliability of someone who has decided that showing up is not optional.

In the days after the accident, Éd was distant in the deliberate way of someone who has decided that emotional availability is no longer part of the arrangement. He checked in minimally. When I said I was in pain, when I said the ribs made breathing uncomfortable, when I said I was scared by what had happened, he responded with the brevity of someone who has found a way to be present without being present.

He never said I'm sorry. Not once. Not about the phone being in his hand. Not about the accident. Not about the women, the child he had not disclosed, the three years.

I lay in bed with my bruised ribs and my bandaged arm and I thought about the woman I had been on a hot August night in her mother's house, scrolling through a dating app. I thought about what she had been hoping for.

The accident didn't change anything. It just made visible what was already true.

He was already gone before the car hit anything. He had been leaving for a long time.

CHAPTER FOURTEEN
Darlene

I need to tell you about my mother. Not as an interruption to the story but as its foundation. You cannot understand the shape of what Édouard was able to do to me without understanding the shape of what I came into the world already carrying.

Darlene Monroe, née Collins, of Savannah, Georgia, is sixty-one years old and has the bone structure of a woman who has been aware of her beauty since childhood and has organized a considerable portion of her identity around it. She is striking — people look at her when she enters rooms, still, at sixty-one, and she knows it and it is part of how she moves through the world. She gave me my face, and for that I am both grateful and complicated.

My mother has Borderline Personality Disorder. A diagnosis she received at fifty and has, in the decade since, handled inconsistently. On good days she is the most insightful person in the room about her own condition. On bad days she rejects the diagnosis entirely and recasts herself as a passionate woman in a world that punishes passion. I have spent my entire life in the space between those two days.

BPD, for anyone who needs context: Borderline Personality

Disorder is characterized by intense emotional dysregulation, unstable relationships, profound fear of abandonment, and a cycle of idealizing and then devaluing the people closest to you. In clinical language it sounds understandable, even sympathetic. In lived experience, as the child of an untreated BPD parent, it sounds like this:

It sounds like being eleven years old and being told you are the most extraordinary child who has ever existed, and then being told at eleven-thirty that you are selfish and ungrateful and the source of everything that has ever gone wrong in your mother's life. Same morning. Same voice. Both delivered with equal conviction.

It sounds like love that arrives in waves so intense they knock you over, followed by withdrawal so complete you forget you were ever warm.

It sounds like a phone call at midnight because she has had a bad memory or a feeling with no name, and she needs you to climb into it with her, and if you cannot — if you are tired or managing your own five children or simply at the end of what you have to give — she will experience your limitation as abandonment. And the abandonment will be real to her. And you will spend the following days trying to repair something you didn't break.

What growing up with her gave me was this: an extraordinary sensitivity to the emotional weather of other people. An ability to read a room that most people don't have access to. A capacity to calibrate my presence in response to someone else's needs that has made me genuinely good at certain things — at being a mother, at my professional work, at being the friend people call in a crisis.

What it also gave me was a trained tolerance for intermittent warmth. A deep-seated belief, installed before I had the language to examine it, that love is conditional and volatile and that the way to keep it is to make yourself useful enough that its withdrawal becomes too costly.

Édouard did not read my psychiatric history. He did not need to. He paid attention for long enough to locate the architecture of my particular susceptibility, and then he built his deception in those exact places.

He found me in my mother's house and he gave me the thing I had spent my whole life not quite receiving: steady, daily, specific attention. The eight a.m. call. The remembered details. The sense of being held in someone's careful consideration.

He gave me my mother's intermittent warmth wrapped in the packaging of consistency. And I, who had been trained since childhood to find that combination irresistible, received it exactly as he intended.

My mother called me on a morning after a difficult night with Éd, and said in that particular tone of hers that sounds like care but is built from control: "I told you about that man."
"You did," I said.
"You never listen to me, Celeste. You have never listened to me."
I held the phone and looked out the window at my children and thought: she is both right and entirely missing the point.
That is the constant truth of my mother: she is often right about the facts and entirely wrong about what the facts require of her.
"I love you, Mama," I said.
She paused. And then, in the softer voice — the one I have been chasing my whole life: "I know. I love you too. You're going to be okay."
I chose to believe her. I have always chosen to believe her when she says this, because in between the difficult, she has always meant it.

CHAPTER FIFTEEN
Four Months Later: The Job, The Snap, The Silence

Four months after the accident, I lost my job.
The accident had consequences. A concussion that made sustained concentration unreliable for weeks. Disrupted sleep that did not fully resolve for months. A low-grade, persistent anxiety that my doctor identified as a trauma response, expressing itself as a difficulty maintaining the kind of focused, high-functioning performance my role at Halloway & Associates required. My instincts were intact. My knowledge was intact. But I was operating at reduced capacity in ways that were not always visible but were sometimes consequential.
A campaign I had been leading underperformed. The post-mortem was professional and courteous and identified gaps in the execution that were traceable, in hindsight, to the specific difficulties I had been managing without disclosing. I had not told my employer about the accident's lasting effects. I had been attempting to manage it quietly and independently, the way I manage most things.
I was laid off on a Thursday morning. Rhonda Halloway sat across from me with genuine regret in the careful lines of her face and said the things that are said in these situations: restructuring, talent not in question, hoped we would work together again in a different context. She meant all of it. That did not change the outcome.

I thanked her. I packed my desk with the efficiency of someone who has learned to function in the middle of catastrophe. I drove home and sat in my driveway for twenty minutes before going inside.

Five children. A mortgage. Two car payments. The immediate mathematics of an income that had just become zero.

I called Éd. I still do not fully understand why. The relationship had degraded so substantially that calling him with anything important had become an act of hope increasingly unsupported by evidence. But I called him, because I was in shock and I needed to tell someone, and he was still the person I had been telling things to for nearly three years, and habit is its own kind of gravity.

"I got laid off," I said.

There was a pause. And then his voice — tight, clipped, carrying an undertone I had been identifying and then un-identifying for three years.

Disgust.

"How does somebody lose their job? That's their own fault. You must have been slipping."

I want you to imagine sitting in your car in your driveway, having just lost your job, and hearing those words from the person you have been with for nearly three years. From the person who has your children's trust. From the person who slept in your bed and ate food from your kitchen and let you drive him to a job interview a week before his phone caused a car accident.

You must have been slipping.

"You have five kids," he continued, with the air of someone delivering a verdict. "You can't afford to slip. You need to figure it out."

Something in me went very still. Not the frightened still. Not the absorbing still. A different kind — the kind that comes when something has been revealed so completely that there is nothing left to protect.

"Don't call me anymore," I said.

I hung up.

He didn't call. He didn't text. For four days, the person who had spent three years calling me every morning at eight o'clock offered no contact whatsoever. No check-in. No acknowledgment of the crisis I was navigating. No revision of what he had said. No apology.

On the fourth day, a text arrived.

I've moved on. You should too.

That was it.

Nearly three years. The daily calls and the Haitian food his mother made and the two years of Saturday mornings in my house with my children. The accident I survived. The hospital. The bruised ribs and the bandaged arm. My brother. All of it — and the closing line was: I've moved on. You should too.

I stood in my kitchen and read that text four times. Then I called my children in for dinner. I made their plates. I listened to Henry's performance of something that had happened at daycare. I helped Amara with her homework. I put Elijah and Zora to bed and sang to Zora the song she needed and sat with Elijah in the quiet way he needed. I held Henry through the tail end of a cold.

I did all of the things I do every single evening, because five people needed me to, and there was no version of this night in which I did not show up for them.

And then I came back to the kitchen, and I allowed myself, for the first time without management or deflection or the usual machinery of my own protection, to feel the full weight of what had happened.

It was heavy. I won't tell you otherwise.

But it had a bottom.

And that was the first thing I had been certain of in a very long time.

PART FOUR

THE BOTTOM AND THE BEGINNING

"You were not made to be small. You were not made to be carried by someone who could barely carry themselves. You were made to rise."
— Morgan Harper Nichols

CHAPTER SIXTEEN
What Surviving Actually Looks Like

People have very particular ideas about what surviving looks like. They expect it to be cinematic — a morning scene, sunlight through curtains, a person gathering themselves from the floor with conviction and visible resolve.

What surviving actually looks like is getting five children to school on time when you have been awake since three in the morning running the numbers and coming up short every time. It looks like calling your insurance company and being on hold for forty-seven minutes and remaining, throughout the entire call, composed and clear-headed and professional. It looks like updating your resume while your chest feels like someone is standing on it.

Surviving is a spreadsheet. A specific, detailed spreadsheet of the next six months built late at night on the kitchen table while everyone else is asleep — that you cannot look at without dread and cannot look away from because the alternative is not knowing.

Surviving is Imani asking if you're sad — Imani, who asks direct questions because she is nine years old and has decided that accuracy is more useful than tact — and you saying I'm a little tired, baby, and her pulling out a book about dolphins without being asked because dolphins, she informs you with the certainty of someone who has researched this, "are proven to make people feel better, statistically."

Surviving is Henry climbing into your lap while you are trying to have a private cry at the kitchen table and grabbing your face in both of his three-year-old hands and announcing, with the urgency of someone delivering critical news: MAMA. HI. I'M HERE.

I laughed. Through the tears, in the kitchen, I laughed until the laughing was bigger than the crying, and Henry accepted this as evidence of a successful performance and returned to whatever he had been doing, satisfied.

That is surviving. Not a single moment of decision. A thousand small recalibrations, daily, in the direction of the life you are responsible for even when the life you are mourning is very loud.

I found new employment within six weeks. A smaller firm — not Halloway's caliber — but a director-level role with a manager named

Sandra Park who had said, in the interview, something that landed: "I hire people, not credentials. Tell me how you think." I told her how I thought for forty-five minutes and she offered me the job the next morning. The salary was less than before. The stability was more.

I negotiated that salary with more resolve than I had negotiated anything in years, because losing something teaches you, sometimes, what the thing was worth.

Dr. Okafor and I had the most honest sessions of our years together in those months. I stopped curating what I brought to her. I told her everything — the Jimmy situation and what it might mean, the multiple women, the phone in the car, the hospital, the text, my brother. I told her about the way I had absorbed and absorbed and called it patience.

"What do you want to understand?" she asked.

"Why I stayed," I said.

"You know why you stayed."

"Yes. But I want to understand it in the place where choices are made. Not just know it — understand it."

She was quiet for a moment.

"Then that's the work," she said.

I did the work. The real, non-cinematic, unsexy, difficult work of sitting with the things I had been running from. Understanding my mother's illness as something that happened to both of us rather than something she did to me. Seeing the pattern without making the pattern my whole story.

I told my children, in age-appropriate ways, that Ed would not be coming around.

Amara said: "I didn't think he was right."

"You could have told me," I said.

"You wouldn't have been ready," she said. Matter-of-fact. Certain.

My eleven-year-old.

Imani cried briefly, because he had taken her animal facts seriously and not many people did that with the full commitment she required. Zora asked if he was going to be okay, because Zora worries about people. Elijah said nothing and then came and sat beside me in the specific Elijah way of wordless companionship. Henry said, with the finality of a three-year-old who has decided: "We don't need him. We have us."

I held Henry for a long time.

Yes, baby. We have us.

CHAPTER SEVENTEEN
The Call From Simone, and Two Fires at the Edges

The call came from a number I didn't recognize, two months after the full ending.

I almost didn't answer. I had developed, in the Édouard years, a habit of not answering unrecognized numbers, because unrecognized numbers had sometimes been unpleasant and I was conserving my capacity for unpleasant things.

Something made me answer.

"Is this Celeste Monroe?"

A woman's voice. Warm, controlled, with a careful quality — braced. The register of someone who has been preparing for this call.

"It is," I said.

A pause. Then: "My name is Simone. I think we need to talk. About Édouard."

We talked for two hours and fifteen minutes. I know the exact duration because I checked my call log afterward.

Simone had been with him for nearly as long as I had, in the specific cycling way I now understood was his method. She had her own version of the sudden coldness, the Jimmy displacement, the nights where the explanation didn't fit the timeline. She had a daughter, two years old. The child I had found referenced in his phone.

I want to be careful about how I describe this conversation, because the narratives available here are ones I am not interested in participating in. Simone was not my enemy. She was not the person who had done anything to me. She was someone who had been lied to in many of the same ways I had been lied to, using many of the same methods, and who had reached out not from competition or blame but from the simple need of someone who wanted their experience witnessed by someone who could fully understand it.

We verified, gently and without cruelty, what we each knew. We filled in each other's gaps. What had been suspicious became confirmed. What had been confirmed became comprehensible as a system — not a series of individual failures but a designed methodology.

At some point in the call she said: "I just needed to talk to someone who wouldn't tell me I was exaggerating."

"You weren't exaggerating," I said.

"Neither were you," she said.

I hung up and sat in my living room and thought about what Dr. Okafor says about healing: that it is not linear, and it is not solitary. That sometimes it requires being witnessed by someone who was in the same room, even if they didn't know each other.

The conversation removed the last operative doubt — the one that says maybe you are the problem, maybe you are too sensitive, maybe a person of more value would have been treated differently. I was not the problem. I had not been too sensitive. My value was not the variable.

Édouard Pierre was the variable. His capacity for sustained, methodical deception — his complete comfort with the cost of it to the people around him — was the variable.

This knowing did not fix everything. But it removed a weight I had been carrying so long I had stopped noticing it had a name.

* * *

By the time summer arrived — my first full season on the other side of Édouard Pierre — I found myself navigating something I had not anticipated.

Two men. Different from each other in almost every measurable way. Both, in their own registers, worthy of attention.

I want to be precise: I did not engineer this. I was a woman who had, after years of investing herself in something fraudulent, found herself in a season of recovery that had, unexpectedly, also become a season of genuine possibility.

Damien Holloway-Cross. Thirty-nine. Atlanta born and raised. Director of Operations at my new firm. I had noticed him in a conference room on a Tuesday morning — not because he was the loudest or most insistent, but because he was genuinely, attentively present in a room full of people who were performing presence. He asked one question in the meeting. He listened to the entire answer before responding. He did not interrupt. He did not check his phone.

When we were introduced after the meeting, he shook my hand with the attentiveness of someone actually registering the person in front of them and said he had heard good things about my work.

"Still rebuilding," I said.

"Most things worth doing take rebuilding," he said.

Over the next several weeks we worked on a shared project. He asked me to lunch — directly, without a secondary language layered underneath the ask: "I'd like to talk through the Meridian direction over lunch. I'd value your perspective outside of a meeting format."

No performance. No angle. Just: here is what I want, stated plainly.

We talked about work for thirty minutes and then, by increments so natural they barely registered as a transition, everything else. He had two children. He spoke about them with the matter-of-fact love of a man who had integrated his children into his identity rather than managing them as a complication. When he disagreed with me — which happened, because we were two people with strong opinions — he said so directly, without aggression, without apology, and then listened to my counter.

A man who tells you plainly when he disagrees with you is not editing himself to maintain your favor. This is significant.

Tobias Greene had been in my life, in the intermittent and uncomplicated way of a first love that ended before it soured, since I was twenty-three. We had met in graduate school, talked until a party emptied around us without noticing, dated for two years. The reason it ended was not dramatic. We were twenty-five and not yet finished becoming ourselves. For years we had stayed in loose, genuine contact. He had attended my grandmother's memorial service. He had sent a thoughtful care package when Henry was born.

He called me in the spring, having heard I had been through something difficult, and asked: "Do you want company that doesn't require you to perform okay?"

"Yes," I said. "I'd like that."

He came on a Saturday and met my children with an ease that was clearly genuine. By the end of the afternoon Amara had spoken to him directly twice, which post-Éd was significant endorsement. Zora declared he was "good" with the authority of someone who has made a final determination.

He said to me, in one of our early conversations back: "I know I wasn't who you needed when we were twenty-five. I think I'm different now. I'm not asking you to take my word for it. I'm asking you to let time show you whether it's true."

I told Dr. Okafor about both of them in the same session.

"How are you feeling about this?" she asked.

"Like I'm standing between two fires," I said. "And both fires are warm. But I know enough now to know that warm and safe are not the same thing. And I'm still learning whether I can tell the difference."

"What would moving toward one of them require?"

"Trusting my own judgment," I said. "Which I am in the process of rebuilding from components."

"What does the rebuilding require?"

"Time. Honesty. Watching rather than deciding. Not letting the

loneliness make the choice before I'm ready."
She was quiet. Then: "That's more than I was going to say."
I am at the beginning of this part of the story. Not at the resolution. At the before — the gathering, the season before the decision that will define the next chapter.
I am thirty years old. I have five children who are my whole heart. I have a job I am growing back into. I have survived a man who borrowed my hope for three years and spent it on other people. I have survived a car accident, a job loss, a text message that was supposed to be a door closing and turned out to be a window opening. I have survived my brother's death and the silence Éd left in the middle of it. And I am still here. Still open. Still, despite all available evidence to the contrary, capable of standing in the warmth of something that might be good and choosing to stay in it long enough to find out.
That is what I am.
The rest is the next book.

EPILOGUE
A Letter to Myself

Dear Celeste,
You are going to want to rush this. You have always wanted to rush the middle. You want to know the ending, the answer, which fire, what the rebuilt life looks like when it is finished.
Stay in the in-between a little longer. The in-between is where the actual information is. It is where you learn who you are when no one is performing for you and you are not performing for anyone. It is where you find out, slowly and without ceremony, whether the thing you are building has a different foundation this time.
You have five children who are watching you live. Not watching you perform living — watching you actually do it, with the full complexity of getting things wrong and correcting and being afraid and going forward anyway. They are storing this. Amara is storing it with her detective's precision. Elijah is storing it in the quiet way he stores everything that matters. Zora will put it in a song one day that she invents herself. Imani will cite it in something factual. Henry will perform it in a living room for an audience that deserves it.
You are giving them the most important thing: evidence that it is possible to be broken and intact at the same time. To be wrong about someone and still trust yourself to try again. To be hurt and still open.

You are not your mother's wounds. You carry them — I will not pretend you don't — but you are not them. You are what grew despite them, which is a different and better thing.

You are not Édouard's version of you. You are not the woman who was useful and then wasn't. That version of you existed only in his accounting, and his accounting was always about himself.

You are Celeste Monroe. You built a career from a woman who started in a one-bedroom house with five children and her mother's complicated love and an eight o'clock call she was beginning to see through. You built a home. You built stability for five people who needed it. You built yourself, slowly and without fanfare, out of the raw materials of everything that tried to diminish you.

There are two men at the edges of your life right now and you don't know what to do with either of them. That's okay. You don't have to know yet. You just have to stay in the story and keep paying attention and trust that the judgment you are rebuilding is already better than the one you started with.

Stay in the story, Celeste.

The best parts are still ahead.

— C.M.

THE BETWEEN TWO FIRES SERIES

SHATTERED CROWNS: The Weight of Beautiful Ruins

SMOKING MIRRORS: The Anatomy of a Soft Lie

THE TENDER INFERNO: When Good Men Burn

BEAUTIFUL DAMAGE: The Price of Being Chosen

CROWNED IN FIRE: A Woman Rebuilt

A PREVIEW OF BOOK TWO
SMOKING MIRRORS: The Anatomy of a Soft Lie

Celeste Monroe thought she had finally learned to read the signs.

Six months out of the wreckage of Édouard Pierre, she has rebuilt enough. Her new job is stabilizing. Her five children are thriving. The slow, necessary work of therapy is doing what it does. She has allowed Damien Holloway-Cross closer, and found in him a steadiness that feels, for the first time in a long time, like something worth standing next to.

She has not allowed herself to stop wondering about Tobias Greene.

Then something in one of those carefully rebuilt dynamics shifts — and the shift has the specific texture of a familiar damage.

SMOKING MIRRORS is the story of the lie that doesn't look like a lie. The one told not with malice but with fear, by someone who believed their own edited version. The one that is warm and well-intentioned and still manages to cost you something you cannot get back. When Celeste discovers that someone she has begun to trust has been less than fully honest about something that matters, she is forced to answer the question she has been circling since the beginning of this story:

How do you trust your own judgment when it has already been wrong?

And what happens when the answer is — you trust it anyway?

Meanwhile, her mother Darlene is unraveling in ways that demand Celeste's presence. And between two men who want her differently, Celeste Monroe must decide not just who to choose — but who she is when she is finally, fully, choosing for herself.

— Available Now in the Between Two Fires Series —

www.ingramcontent.com/pod-product-compliance
Lightning Source LLC
LaVergne TN
LVHW012340100826
845148LV00018B/3222

* 9 7 9 8 9 0 4 1 7 6 9 3 8 *